When Time Waited

Published By

When Time Waited

Written by Bhanuprakash Singh

Copyright ©

Bhanuprakash Singh - POETRY WORLD ORG 2021

ISBN (Paperback) – 978-93-90724-04-8

First Edition : 2021

Book Design by POETRY WORLD

When Time Waited

Written By

Bhanuprakash Singh

Introduction

When we intend to do something very strongly, though it may seem impossible at first, it will come to life one day. Our strength and our belief, our dream and our vision, our projection of how we want to be, all rely on the truth for which we stand in our life. Emotions always find a place in each of us in several forms, and to me, writing is that.

This book is a collection of poems penned down from the observations around, from the stories that surround, from the freedom that keeps us bound, and from each life that strives for success, writing a story so profound! And every word that flowed from my pen, was a thought from my heart.

Holding this book, I wish to invite you into the world of emotions and for that time when you pass along my lines, forever you are my emotion too!

Acknowledgement

To my dear wife, whose support is soulful and whose love is endless

> Far across the distance,
>
> miles along hand in hand,
>
> You walk beside,
>
> be journey any land!
>
> Alone which, on this side,
>
> I'd never see a chance!

To my editor and publisher, who worked best to bring this book to life!

To my creator, who is everywhere but never elsewhere!

Dedicated to you who gave your precious time

for this book!

I owe you from my heart!!

INDEX

THE SONG

In my tune, lies life,

the melody so high,

the peace calming does lie!

What's with you, that's more?

In my words, lies meaning,

the purpose of this being,

where reality, convincingly will cling!

What's with you, that's more?

In my tune, lies science,

the way of blessing disguised,

the heart soothing, so nice!

What's with you, that's more?

In my words, lies belief,

the teachings of nature hidden,

and thoughts of greatest visions!

What's with you, that's more?

Dear lyric, who does care?

Your words are bizarre!

neither they go to commonaire,

nor bring a calmness fair!!

Dear music, who does need

your tunes? nothing for good indeed!

neither a meaning to plead,

nor a thought one can heed!

Dear lyric, let's test our worth!

Dear music, let's test, be no dearth!

(Lyric plays)

Man: Music it does lack!

(Music plays)

Man: Lyrics were to back?!

Dear, we are worth nothing!!

Neither do you, nor I bring

any cheer in this being!

Together if we could cling,

his science will make him sing!

AT THAT DOOR

That haunts me, thy need!

Do you ever have to plead

or, ever have to boast your deed?

Do you ever have to lead

the herd of ghosts indeed?

When you've all that you need,

why this crave be your feed?

That haunts me, thy need!

Where have been, those serene

and to play, the places of green?

Where have the silent thoughts been,

whose memories', stronger than they seem?

When you know these paths to lean

Why this unrest be your bean?

That haunts me, thy need!

How have you ever been there,

where you thought was not thy share?

How have you ever walked dare,

and rejected those demons of scare?

When you've seen the horizon bare,

why this greed do you care?

That haunts me, thy need!

Life's a one-time knock at the door

and you grabbed it very sure

to live away from lifeless, more!

While living you sunk this ship, washed ashore!

You have fallen, risen like never before!

But why have you again been waiting at that door??

THE HIDDEN INTENTION

The morning's so fresh!
The rising sun calls me,
peeking into my dreams free!
Wanting its beauty, my eyes see,
it rushes through, unto me!

The morning's so fresh!
The chirping birds so sing,
the tunes that happiness' bring!
Wanting its music, in my ears ring,
they hover over, for me awaiting!

The morning's so fresh!
The greens of the farms rise,
to reach the morning lights!
Wanting its excitement, I praise,
they dance swaying to amaze!

The morning's so fresh!
The dews from nowhere remind,
that they too are in task behind!
Wanting my reaction, they bind
all that's in sight, to me freshness they rewind!

The morning's so fresh!
The breeze gently touches my face,
and awakens me to morning's haze!
Wanting me to close my eyes and gaze,
that all I long to, so poetry I phrase!

The morning's so fresh!! Oh!! The morning's so fresh!!!

HE HAS RISEN

From the plagues of ignorance,
and though noxious the offense,
He has risen, has risen hence,
the belief, that we all can be friends!

From the homes of hopelessness,
and treats of the rich, pushing illness,
He has risen, has risen to harness,
the hope, that we all embrace oneness!

From the droughts of losses,
and the time's alike wars of roses,
He has risen, has risen to prove us,
the faculty of realization, what within does!

From the dreams of the deadly,
and the frightens of what tomorrows be,
He has risen, has risen to free,
the thoughts of yet another catastrophe!

He has risen, be from within,
or from the hopes far seen.
He has risen, be from emptiness,
or from the eyes of awareness.

He, that energy, that freedom!
He, for what your life awaits!
He is that being, hidden in you,
who has risen, though buried,
for what your birth was agreed!!

Together, Profound be thy deed!

GAZER OF THE GHAST

The tree knows it all!!
From the ages of freshness,
till the bad times that harness.
From the lands of its brethren,
till the families of its ridden.

The tree knows it all!!
From the days of meetings,
under the shadows of its wings,
till the times of those things,
written on its flesh and skins.

The tree knows it all!!
From the worships of its presence,
thanking the sacredness dense,
till the worships of those idols,
carved of its breath, lying at itself.

The tree knows it all!!
From those matters that care,
till those matters who care.
From those moments of splendor,
till those of humane blunder.

The tree's seen it all,
standing right here still tall,
silent are its cries, dry are its tears,
will not it retaliate, or die in fear!
But one day, we too shall know it all!

A CHANGE FOR GOOD

It is not what we want,

that from which all's lost,

and know of no past.

Happened just like a glow,

not but glorious, put us low.

It is not what we want,

that caused this distance,

disturbed the very balance.

Happened just in the flow,

not but noticed, put us low.

It is not what we want,

that ceased the normal,

and the function stall.

Happened just hard as a blow,

not but learned, put us low.

It is not what we want,

that death from nowhere,

eat us swiftly, and spread where?

Happened just like fear,

not but realized, put us low.

It is not what we want,

but it is we who taunt,

this very nature, and flaunt,

big is humanity while it won't.

It is what we are thus, brought

by it, at our doorstep unsought.

It is what that is born of actions,

that withheld care and beheld greed.

Be known,

Round is the globe, so is life!

So does the day shine after the night!

And we too from sleep shall rise bright!

But that day and beyond, we as a humanity

MUST CHANGE!!

IN THAT YOU

In you, let dwell,
the strength to have sorrow dispel!
Let the skies of dawns spread
cheer and blossom ahead!

In you, let live,
the smiles of pure, attractive!
Let the breeze of freshness
gently tease and life harness!

In you, let shine,
the thoughts of care pristine!
Let the horizons insight,
keep the sorrows of life tight!

In you let grow,
the child of tomorrow!
Let the leaves of spring,
cast nature's way of wellbeing!

In that you, my dear,
I shall rest afar my fear,
and lie of thought cleared!
For those moments of peace,
will leave, I, what is near,
and within too,

In that YOU!

LET ME BE ME

In the oceans heavy,
and among the choices many,
force not me, into what you see!
Push not me, in that you be!
For once, let me be me.

In the tufts of grass aplenty,
and the flowers full of honey,
stress, not me, to earn a penny!
Drive not me, to luxuries sundry!
For once, let me be only.

Midst the fogs of morning rays,
as the dew of freshness lays,
guide not me, through your ways!
Hold not me, where lifeless are days!
For once, let me rephrase.

Hovering like the clouds so shy,
hiding in, the energies so high,
leave not me, in a race to die!
Lie not to me, beyond smiles do lie!
For once, let me alone try.

Be what the worlds around,
and how the success' may sound,
Hail me but by what you're bound,
in a world, that I built so sound!
By letting me be me, for once...abound!!

TOO FAR

The hands that held tight,
led the way, all so bright,
but what lasts ever?
After the light, darkness does shower!

The shoulders that bore the might,
cared nothing in all the fight,
but what lasts ever?
when there's a win, the loss too shall bother!

The steps that made things right,
stood never be any hurdle in sight,
but what lasts ever?
That which can stand, bound to fall over!

The words that drove far the plight,
said a million things, built courage's height,
but what lasts ever?
Where build the courage, beneath lies fear!

The eyes that watched over as a wright,
to mold a life, to which, worlds await,
but what lasts ever?
Where the eyes can see, that exists never!

Nothing you think lasts forever,
One day shall see the loss cover,
that what you think was for granted,
and all you can do is to ponder over,
ways to fill that emptiness, which, however,
shall happen never!!

because, that's gone, and just gone too far!
that life is just gone very far!!

LET GO

Let go, all that in you,
with what you never knew,
that known, thus to a few,
the wise men! You hence let go!

Let go, all that in you,
with what you think is your own,
that which, thus be torn,
after you! You hence let go!

Let go, all that in you,
with what you build all pride,
that with which, even they stride
not, the gods! You hence let go!

Let go, all that in you,
that which you think is you,
clouded in it you never renew,
that which is true! You thus let go!

Let go that is near and dear,
but by it, you know no fear!
Let go of all that fire and desire,
by it, you live a step higher!

Let go that you aspire and admire,
by it, you are a debonaire!
Let go of what may be the tire,
in peace, if you wish to retire!!

AM I THAT I FORESEE?

A thousand thoughts, and a gallon fears,

lie in me, while I lead this life meres.

A boulder burdens, and louder shears,

stay with me, while I show no tears.

Am I, doing that doing, that needs me to be done?

A multitude of scars, and a barren way of mars,

seen to mine, while I journeyed across wars.

A sea of chars, and shadowed lights to fars,

seem to me, luring towards sailless spars.

Am I going there, going, where I need be gone?

A cloud of doubts, and rain of curious cases,

show to me, a flood's never worthy till ceases,

A sky of thoughts and vastier be the teases,

that fly in me, but I never see any diseases.

Am I thinking that thinking, that needs me to be

thought?

A deep valley of falls, and a rushing flow of wonders,

though thrushling in me, I fail to their ponders.

A mountain of the unknown, and a fountain of known,

dares

me to be known by that known, while unknown none

cares!

Am I knowing that unknown, that needs me to be
known?

Am I doing this to be done, by the means to be?
Am I or, going nowhere, singing winnings' lullaby?!
Am I or, thinking this, to be taught to me?
Am I or, re-knowing only known, though unknown I see?!
If thinking, to doing the deeds, beyond the might of the
sea,
to know the unknown is right,
I will keep going! That I foresee!

Am I but,
right on a wrong way, or wrong on a right way?
If right on a wrong way I am, I hope nothing!
If wrong on the right way I am, I wish nothing!!

A FIGHTER

What cost me my pain,
lies in me in no vain.
From it, shall I all gain,
let there be more such rain!

What cost me this stain,
shows to me my disdain!
From it, shall I train,
let there be more such rain!

What cost me from world, hain,
stays in me for to frain!
From it, shall I rise again,
let there be more such rain!

There shall be no such pain,
that outshines the will of mine!
From all that I can, I shine,
let there be any such rain,
as a fighter...
in the pages, I will remain!!

THEY WILL TELL YOUR TALES

Why should I learn?

Shall I do to earn a ton?

Shall I do to bear that burn?

Shall I do it for a bun?

Or, shall I do it for fun?

How do I learn?

Do lot, I have to read?

Do I have to rope that greed?

Do I have to cope to thy need?

Or, Do I have to plot a seed?

What should I learn?

Shall I learn what's in?

Shall I learn what's seen?

Shall I learn how to live happy?

Or, Shall I learn how to 'leave' better?

Confused am I, Confused is my soul?!!

They say, I have to learn.

They say, today will not return.

They say, if I don't like all, run,

useless I'll be, ever undone.

And when my eyes all wet,

they jest and have fun!

They, filled whole in me,

They, whom I never see,

They, control all of me,

They, whose faces never shall be.

They, live entire in me,

They, who know no sea!!

I will only, thus learn,

to grow from within dearn,

though that sun thinks, can burn,

shadow and protect I will thy haven,

and blossom from within in turn,

spreading color, even when fallen upturn,

fruits for hungry, I shall bestow with concern!!

Deeds of these, be tales they share,

those who think, I could make it nowhere!!

HAVE YOU KNOWN EVER?

Have you known ever?
What comes, will remain never!
What remains, is worthy never!
What's worthy, is heeded never!

Have you known ever?
Which you own, exists never!
Which you want, never is near!
Which you think is near, isn't dear!

Have you known ever?
Whose help you need, is within!
Who's within, nobody knows!
Who's known, never can seep within!

Have you known ever?
That you dream is never the future!
That future is known by no thought,
that thought which forms, only by the present!

Have you known ever?
To love whole is only worth!
To own nothing is only rich!
To know the within is supreme knowledge!!

Have you known ever?
To be, thus, is the only truth!
To grow, thus, is the only route!
To leave better, thus, the only chore!

A BOW TO SELFLESS

Been to hilltops, seen your shrines!
Been to tiny huts, seen your love!
Been to mighty homes, seen your grace!
Yet I never know why this disgrace!

Been to the woods, felt life so fresh!
Been to seas, knew your strength!
Been to valleys, felt your omniscience!
Yet I never know why this disgrace!

Been to countries, knew your forms!
Been to libraries, read your deeds!
Been to retreats, dwelled in deeps!
Yet I never know why this disgrace...

Oh the creator, the energy of you
this world shall never know.
This disgrace....why then do you undergo,
that which we, of selfishness, bestow?!

It's good, all that you do!
The world shall never though know,
that smiles are not milestones to row.
There are things beyond & we ought to bow!!

THE STAGE

The tears, let flow!
The sorrow, let grow!
The heart, be it low!
Shall you strive not,
never shall you thrive lot!!

The games, let lost!
The race, let last!
The spirit, be on fast!
Shall you revive not,
never shall you relive lot!!

The fears, let haunt!
The moments, let daunt!
The mind, be bold not!
Shall you master it not,
never shall you reap from, lot!!

The scars, let lay!
The grue, let play!
Life, be a pity not!
Shall you rise not,
Never wise your thought!

If life's a play just,
to win or lose, thus a jest.
Why thee then be, in this dust
and let gloom be thy guest!

To act and to leave, be the way best
rather watch it just
and
later lie to rest!!

WHATEVER IT TAKES

May the darkness tame,
So be the Lord's game.
Bestow on me all blame,
though none of my deed,
will hurt thy self indeed!

May the skies cloud,
so be the rains loud,
flood on me all the bould,
though none of my thought,
will put thy self unsought!

May the buds not bloom,
so be the garden's gloom,
blossom on me all doom,
though none of my sight,
will see thyself fight!

Mine is a mind shallow,
deep within, but may not show.
Mine is a heart, borrow!
Far in you, so no sorrow!
One day but, may you know,
All that will be your's,
Son! Today I shall sow...

..

....

......Whatever it takes..!!

RISE TO LIFE

The world shall rise one day,
to the sunrise, like today,
that which shall lift my brethren,
from the shallows of greed, but when??

The world shall rise one day,
to the fresh air, like today,
that which shall, from hell to heaven,
transform their tiring life, but when??

The world shall rise one day,
to the night's light, like today,
that which can guide the darkened,
notion of happiness, but when??

The world shall rise one day,
to the infants smile, like today,
that which can borne hopes of thousand ten,
for a future so pure as its eyes can see, but when??

The world shall rise one day,
to the morning's dew, like today,
that which can melt as if life taken,
yet, lives in thoughts of peace, but when??

The world shall rise one day,
to the sweet nectar, like today,
that which can bring out all hidden,
the real beauty not but the flower alone, but when??

To that day shall we wait,
or bring it fore, for to wait,
is tying thy wings whose only trait,
wants us to fly beyond, to that world,
where we rise to live and not strive to!!

LET'S DO IT

To the universe, must be tomorrow

To you or me, it but never has a vow.

One day shall remain never, to shadow

the thought of doing just tomorrow!

To the might of his creation must be rebirth

To you or me, it but never gives hope.

One life is a gift from depths, to rope

in all that takes to return the best to that which is reborn!

To the good, must be all brighter

To you or me, it but never may throw light.

One deed or a million, for good things a fight

will always make way for that dream, just at sight!

To the universe, there must be tomorrow

To you or me, it can yet bring a vow

that in a deed of goodness or a work of purpose

to this creation, we shall ever live in the beauty of its

existence!

DUST THAT DARK

The dark clouds above
engulf me and show
though light all around sow,
it doesn't matter for it though
because night always is there
and darkness more, it can borrow!

I still can find some light
and fight against it might
I can walk and can still be right
and no night can stop this fight.
I see far and beyond a nightmare
and in me a hope, farther than sight!

The heavy pour down now
drenched me to show
gone is my light, least I now bow,
to that darkness, my foe!
But I didn't and against I dare
for, my hope runs from head to toe!

I still walked, determined as past
and tore the darkness that cast,
for, how long can its fight last!
I soon saw the light vast,
ousting all darkness and none to spare
for a man whose desire to win just
was all he could lust
and never adjust..!

WITHIN, YOU MUST FIND

A piece of peace
is all I need to fleece
my inner self, in a slice
of calm and frozen silence.
Can I get it in the temple, Oh Lord?

A moment of freshness
is all I need to harness
my thought even in darkness
of falter and fall's tameness.
Can I get it among this nature, Oh Lord?

A heart of love
is all I need to know
my strength in caring a foe
& that brotherhood I shall pursue.
Can I get it in your creation, Oh Lord?

Oh, dear beauty!..MY Beauty!
What you wish is within,
What you long is within,
What you need is within.

That peace is in your mind!
That freshness is in your thought!
That love is in your heart!
So, Can you get it all, Oh Man??

THE UN-... WAY OF LIFE

The wheel, the fire, and no end to desire.

The comfort, the pleasure, and all too higher,

we dreamt and built, in disguise, a drier

world of brutal remains of dire and

this gift of life is now endangered!!

The trees, the rivers, and no end to hunger.

The deeds, this living, and all too longer

we did and built, in disguise, a wronger

future filled with the gift of greed to garner and

this gift of nature is now endangered!!

The birds, the animals, and no end to prejudice.

The growth, the need, and all for a price

we did and built, in disguise, the wise

culture drenched in foolishness to raise and

this gift of kith and kin is now endangered!!

The world around was built and poured

in with life to enjoy the blessing bestowed!

To sustain that life, the seeds of green sowed

and to feed them indeed, the rivers were rowed!

When the ultimate beauty is the gift of life itself,

See!! where have we alone had shown???!!

SOLITUDE... CAN I BE?

I am going where, with
all this on my shoulder?
Do I need kin and kith
or can alone I be bolder?
I know no one while birth
and I know left none, where other
never had a tear for his death.

I am going where, with
all this on my mind?
Do I need a laugh and a talk
or alone I be a friend, within bind?
I know no one who had a walk
without a hand around the neck wind
talking such that nothing's left dark.

I am going where, with
all this in my heart?
Do I need love and a heart for all
or alone can I be a lover too?
I know no one who stood all tall
without a stroke of love, fresh as dew
even after nothing left beyond all that fall.

When I know none who are free
of the thought of brotherhood,
of the thought of friends who stood,
of the thought of lover who could,
in any time be your side just to be
so that one never will be where one is,
can I go where I need to go
with the thought of being a solitary reaper!!

SOULFUL ME

I need no time
I need no wine
I need no shrine
But one way to shine...

I need no trace
I need no says
I need no race
but one way to brace...

I need no wheel
I need no deal
I need no reel
but one way to appeal...

I need no song
I need no strong
I need no wrong
but one way to go long...

I need to shine through me
I need to brace the inner me
I need to appeal to me
that I can go long ....not only with me....!!!

AND JUST LIKE THAT...WILL BE GONE

In a split of time
it has away and gone,
leaving me no rhyme,
I felt it was way too wrong.

In a matter of a moment
its task was all done.
Only to plunge the torment
I felt it was born!

In the blink of my eye
it seeked its alternate hive
neither it had mercy nor a sigh of shy
that I felt no good's more alive!

In a thought just born
it stole that fear to don
and show me how it was torn
I felt all gloom to borne!

Where there's life, shall be death!
Where there's boon, shall be dearth!
And now that known to be true,
I shall rise above and find that virtue
of a life that's to be lived well....for this blessing is no
more disguise!

THEY

What occurred to me

usually occurs in the sea

burdens inside and roaring out

but they say, it's dancing without a doubt.

What occurred to me

usually happens in the clouds

stopping heat and harm, showing hope

but they say, in need, it will never rope.

What occurred to me

usually occurs to everyone

fighting battles within and marching through

but they say, that is life and its true

But, Who are 'they' who we think that say,

and to whom we surrender our sway

and in whose conscience we try to stay,

what occurred to me, a question of 'they',

has ever occurred to you any day??

And does freedom lie beyond 'they'??

OH, MR. SUNSHINE

Oh, Mr. Sunshine,

why do you light the dark

and show me the world all

the one that never knew and

the one that can never know,

dark is their light and in light

they keep the dark alive.

Oh, Mr.Sunshine,

Why do you still light the dark

lending the never-ending wars within

in a form to enlighten the war amongst,

the one who only knew and

the one that can only know,

war is their birthright and its end

can lend the land to one alone, unlike you.

Oh, Mr.Sunshine,

You can ever shine and grow like the wine

but all you expect from your light

is all a myth but please realize

what's within you, is within us too.

Like a mother, you bear your brunts

to light us all, and like no other

we survive to stand against fall.

Oh, Mr. Sunshine,

Please shine not and let dark prevail,

this light from you is misused

and dare you to complain any day,

but I know, you never will do

for, your hope is that of a mother

and your burning pain too.

Oh, Mr.Sunshine,

Humanity is all hence, due

Ignorant of the plight behind

their sight of the path but blind!

What Irony...what an irony Mr.Sunshine!!!

AN OLD FOLKLORE

Silently flows the river, no gush..no rush
Birds chirping some old folklore fly above thus
Amidst lost in myself I feel the nature hush
to allow it take along, a lost son in an urban fuss!
Admiring I close my eyes and breathe green lush,
calling nature to surrender and heal me as it does!

In her care and love, I had my sorrows smush
and every breathe danced to the inner opus
in harmony with songs of neighboring thrush
in the night sky, my life shone like the venus!
The truth of living in freedom of thought is the brush
to paint the portrait of life and shall be, she said, the
magnum opus!!

And healed and built, I returned beside the silent rush
of the river to open my eyes...to catch the next bus
Leaving her back and building an aura of deep slush
I return to the same old chaos of the urban fuss
but reformed for a serene living and all foolishness flush!

To gift life back with more than what it gave us!!

A FOSSIL IN THE FROST

A small element I am,

To no one's reach, I can travel

neither do any one's thought, I disturb.

A warrior within I am,

To no one's rage, I can fight

neither do any one's might, I relate.

A minute idea I am,

and to no one's mind, I can occur

neither do any one's imagination, I intrude.

A sole reaper I am,

To no one's growth, I can compare

neither do any one's prosperity, I interrupt.

Then why do all, after all, feel I am lost

and see me a fossil in frost?

And how do I tell them all

I have a life vast and along I wouldn't want to fall??

I WILL SEE YOU

At the shore......

I await to see you,

coming on the waves rushing to me.

With every breeze that touches me,

I see a hope swaying to meet you.

The moon too lightens a path

for you to ride along back, soon.

Also, it lightens my eyes awaiting, and

I see a hope swaying to meet you.

Every wave rushing unto me

wants you to come to me...

All energy they ingress to make us one,

yet the sun in my day never has shown.

I sent you letters in bottles,

I called your name in echoes,

I saw hope on the horizon.....

....All but came back, and never was my sun shown...

They say, *"The ocean is vast.*

And thus your man must be lost"

But in my ocean of love, you never were lost...

This is much smaller and so I know, I will see you!

I will see you, I know...

I will see you, you know...

And if the ocean is what

that makes us apart,

along with you, in its heart,

I too shall become a part.

At the shore...

I still await to see you...

And my dear,

In every fight of life,

I am with you...

THE PHENOMENA OF HOPE

The alarm rings, while I am in deep sleep.

The birds sing, the song of dawn in me to seep...

The breeze flows, to convey the freshness to seek...

The leaves cut air, make music and say their strength in
being sleek...

The prayer far off reminds me the morning sun is at its
peak...

And I am yet asleep, afraid of yet another day to sneak...

To live is to live your love, or each day away from me life
would take...

But the hope when every morning as all the forces speak
....

Builds up the day to push into the next, and phenomenal
it turns

That one day, you will talk to me, and beautiful will be all
my burns!!!

ABHORRENCE

A man was on the floor
Selling coco at the shore.
Making meal & money, he's happy.
Looking at the stars, he laid airy.
But the tale had a twist
With no legs, he held tight his fist
And the hatred tale started.

His fingers ran through pages
He knew history since sages
Giving lectures he spent the day
Moon or sun, knowing not from where came the ray
There lied in the tale a twist
With no eyes, he held tight his fist
And the hatred tale started.

In a garden bloomed a flower
The reason being aroma, all wanted it ever
Few hours hence, it was plucked
Days later, dry it looked
That is where the tale took a twist
This' one more in that list
And the hatred tale started.

The hatred tale that had a twist
When few couldn't hold tight their fist
That hatred tale still in place
When some flawed life as they couldn't race
When a man wins if he thinks he can
& flower that spreads cheer before it dries
WHY SHOULD A LOSER END LOSER??

THE MANGO TREE

That mango tree was no normal

It got immense love so mortal

From dawn to dusk he watered

Hoping it is never left shattered

Plucking the fruits at noon

He sat by it with all bloom.

That mango tree is no normal

It got immense love so mortal

What is it that brings that bloom

In this man, so fat and hair so white

Was the thought that always rung

When I usually see him sing.

That mango tree is no normal

It got immense love so mortal

My lady love sowed this seed

and fed to it her life

I cried, cried and I cried

And one day she grew up

Through ground and this is it

He said with a whisper.

That mango tree is no normal

It got immense love so immortal

Telling his tale of love

He had the last mango from it

He bore a smile on his face

A tear in each eye

The seed in his palm.

That mango tree is no normal

It got immense love so mortal

Despite it being watered

Although I gave utmost care

In no time it became dry

And in the air remained only their love.

FOR IT NEVER CAME BACK

I stood by the silence of its breath
I looked at the flower of its wreath
For it never came back
since I cared it not!!

I stood by the shade of its hands
I looked at the strength of its strands
For it never came back
since I fed it not!!

I longed for a taste of its fruits
I looked for the dance of its leaves
For it never came back
since, for long, never I was back!!

It longed my return but I didn't
It looked from the past but I didn't
It stood for the future but I didn't
Dry it though grew
and flourished it never

I now stand by it
For it is no more.
I should have cared it
For it wasn't my bungle!!

The trait of a man
to love not the one
who loves him a ton
had cost me, my love
For it was such a love

A human, perhaps, could never bestow!!

FOR MY FUTURE

I knew nothing about me
until, as a boy, I hurt my knee
I cried, stood, walked to see
the pain as mighty as the sea
while my courage as small as a bee
I bore it to it remain a pain

I knew nothing of me
until, as a teen, I hurt my heart
I hoped, pleased, begged in distort
My love, I carried in a cart
had wheels that fell apart
I bore it to it remain a dream

I knew nothing of me
until, as a man, I was held responsible
I explained but to none was plausible
The trust they laid on thy being able
affluently begot the world of effluable
I bore it to it remain a lesson

I knew nothing of me
until I faced in life the trouble
That never on me was subtle
Ionely knew to preach him rumble
Through the life's tremble
Yes! This was all perhaps for my son!

BOOMERANG

Nature has a language
that I and you can age and age
but never know or image
until there are effects of her rage!

Nature has given much
that I and you care not as such
but there will be a day we touch
when there's left nothing much!

Nature has beauty unbound
that I and you never look around
and rebuild our own, proper and sound
but in ways wrong, that'll come round!

Nature has a million kids and more
that I and you exploit therefore
and think all is our's that we explore
but the sea throws all that trash, back at the shore!

Nature, so vast and diverse
built families and colors to immerse
and we think we are the universe
unknowing it is in nature, we finally converse!
What a fool of ourselves, we have made reverse!!

THIS IS WORLD

I can't rise to the need
neither best is my deed
and never I pay a heed
because I best be at my speed!

I can't care to any wish
neither it bothers to establish
anything that holds me sluggish
because I have richness to fish!

I can't be by any side
neither I can surf the tide
that slows my race to pride
because I have the best roads to ride!

I can't cry for what you lost
neither I can work without a cost
and nothing I gain being thy host
because I have works hundred almost!

You may say I am selfish and more,
and this world says they don't adore!
But the truth is dear,
this is the world and its age-old folklore!!

FOURTH DIMENSION

I need a lifetime to know
this world that's so ahead
a lightyear at least somehow,
but detached heart to head!

I need a lifetime to learn
how all around compete to run
a race that never they yearn,
but fake happiness bright like the sun!

I need a lifetime to see
what is with my own that longs
and where this herd takes me,
but a question points me all wrongs!

I need a lifetime to digest
the strangeness in a present
that is wasted in ways best
but never we care about any consent!

I need a lifetime, probably another too
and also more than just two
and after that too, will I ever ?!
Perhaps it requires dimension another!!

SEASONS OF LIFE

There have been seasons many
the fall, the spring, and other any!!

Walking past the lanes of memory,
it was easy to stay yet a worry,
where I wish stayed, will I be alone?
like the trunk that stood when fall!!

Going beyond the bonds of the heart
where cozy I lay, I went apart
what I left behind, still my own?
like the leaves that left during fall!

Flying into the dreams set far
where smiles worth all the scar,
had I forgot what longings are?
like the branches that wait after fall!

If the spring can bring the new
and freshness all around it can renew
Can I too find the trunk that bear?
Can I blossom and beauty be shared?

THAT DAY

It is not far, that day

be known!

To do things of heart,

it is never late to start

and rise above limits, hard!

Universe existed and it will.

It is not far, that day

be known!

To bring smiles on loved,

spread a word, hug and hold

and with you, let be bold!

Universe exists and it will...

It is not far, that day

be known!

To lend a hand that cares,

give it now, or those mares

don't mind giving those, their shares!

Universe exists, it will....

It is not far, that day

be known!

To do what makes you human,

you care all, though does no-one,

in return that gets you done!

Universe exists, it will....

It is not far, that day

be known!

Do that you are here for, be dare

Row hardships for smiles you care

Sow seeds whose fruits, all share

Be human that in you world shall adore

Universe existed, will exist...

Not shall we, be known

It is not far, that day!

61

62

www.ingramcontent.com/pod-product-compliance
Lightning Source LLC
LaVergne TN
LVHW051511170726
843492LV00002B/873